The Fabrics of Fairytale

To my father who told me stories and my mother who taught me to sew — T. R. B.
For Betzy and Robert, and with thanks to Jo — R. G.

Barefoot Books
2067 Massachusetts Ave
Cambridge, MA 02140

This book is printed on 100% acid-free paper

Graphic design by Jennie Hoare, Bradford on Avon
Color separation by Grafiscan, Verona
Printed and bound in China by Printplus Ltd

This book was typeset in Minion 13.5pt
The illustrations were prepared in embroidered collage on handmade papers
Paperback ISBN 978-1-84686-089-8

Library of Congress cataloging-in-publication data is available upon request

3 5 7 9 8 6 4

The Fabrics of Fairytale

Stories spun from far and wide

collected and retold by

Tanya Robyn Batt

illustrated by

Rachel Griffin

Barefoot Books
Celebrating Art and Story

Contents

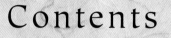

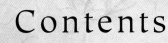

Contents

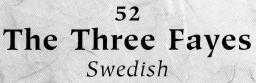

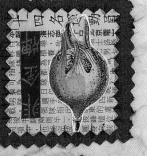

Introduction

Once upon the warp and weft of woven worlds, when laces and brocades adorned the earth, when the day sky was royal blue satin and the night sky dark crumpled velvet…enfolded amid the hills and valleys of these worlds was a place where weavers and wordsmiths, seamstresses and storytellers gave life to the fabrics of fairy tale.

The telling of tales and the making of fabrics are both fundamental human activities, for they both express the desire to marry the ordinary with the fabulous. And of course, in the carding and spinning of wool, the weaving of cloth and the dyeing of yarn, gossip, jokes and the songs and stories of generations and cultures have always been exchanged. But what did our ancestors talk about? What did they care about? Historically, what we know of previous civilizations has been pieced together from bone, clay, metal and stone. The study of history through textiles is difficult, as cloth is so inherently prone to decay. The earliest remnants we know of date from 3000 BC and were recovered from Scandinavian bogs. However, the craftsmanship evident in these fabrics indicates that weaving and the production of cloth had already been mastered for a much longer period of time. The first looms date to around 6000 BC but the simple belt loom, which is still used today in Central and South America, may well have existed several thousand years prior to this. It is worth considering how much more we might know if we were able to follow the flaxen or cotton, silken or golden thread back through the ages.

The production of cloth is so widespread that most cultures contain written or oral records documenting a deity, usually a goddess, who was associated with fabric production. The Dogon peoples of Mali attribute the creation of all things to spinning and weaving activities. Their mythology talks of the Seventh Ancestor Spirit using her face to weave the world, with eight spools of cotton falling from her mouth. For the ancient Greeks, the goddess Athene presided over the art of weaving as well as the art of pottery. And in India, Visvakarma, the divine architect of the universe, is the object of devotion for craftspeople of all kinds.

Today, synthetic fibers have become commonplace in the industrialized nations, but cloth can be created from a huge variety of plant and animal fibers. Some of the most common materials are cotton, silk, wool, flax and hemp. In most societies, the lot of fabric production primarily falls to women. Typically, women are the spinners and weavers, the creators of home furnishings and clothing. However, in those societies where the cloth production is marked by the division of domestic and commercial use, the master weavers and craftspeople are nearly always men.

Traditionally, different cultures and the social and professional substrata within them have identified themselves through the choice of material, the production techniques, and the patterns and designs on the fabrics they make and wear. However, the character of different fabrics also reflects the meetings between the different peoples of the world. Textiles have always been an important trade commodity and many international relationships have been built upon the trading of silk and cotton. In many countries, textiles stand as a testament to cultural exchange, whether in the form of an adopted weaving technique, a new dye, or the combining of an Eastern tree of life with the English country garden, as depicted on Indian cotton prints.

Fabrics have a multiplicity of uses. They have a functional purpose, to warm and protect; they are used for transportation and for furnishings as well as for clothes; they denote status and power; and they are central to the spiritual and ceremonial rituals of many people. The embroidering of an intricate prayer shawl; the stitching, crocheting and weaving of items for the trousseau; the wrapping of bodies in funeral shrouds; and the passing of a feather cloak down through the generations — each of these gestures and garments says something to us about what it means to be human. And of course, each of them has its story to tell. So turn the page and let yourself enjoy the weaving and wearing of stories, where the warp is that which is constant and unchanging and the weft is the bright and darkly colored threads whose dance creates vivid patterns and intricate designs. These are the threads that give shape, color and texture to our lives. These are the fabrics of fairy tale.

Tanya Robyn Batt

Carpet weaving in the Caucasus & Persia

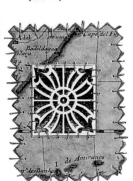

Since earliest times, fine rugs have been woven in Armenia and other countries of the Caucasus. Each country, and each region, developed its own particular style. And from the third century AD, when Persia started to dominate their country, Armenian carpet makers adopted many features of Persian carpet making.

The nomadic tribes of Persia and the Caucasus use wool from camels, goats and sheep to make their carpets. Sheep's wool is most commonly used, but goat and camel hair, silk and cotton are often added to give both strength and variation in texture. The carpets are usually knotted, or take the form of a flat-woven "kilim," like the carpet woven in this story by King Vachagan and his fellow captives. There are two kinds of knotted carpet: those that use Persian and those that use Turkish knots. Turkish knots are more common in the Caucasus. The more knots per inch, the better the carpet.

Traditionally, carpet fibers were colored using natural sources, such as tree roots, leaves, lichens and even insects — indigo for blue, cochineal or madder for red, and the reseda plant or saffron crocus for yellow. The color green (produced

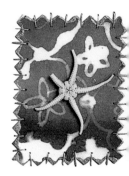

by mixing blue and yellow dyes) was used sparingly as it is the sacred color of Islam.

The carpets are woven on either a horizontal or a vertical loom. Nomadic tribespeople prefer the vertical loom as it is lighter and can be collapsed and carried on the back of a camel. However, every time the loom is moved, the warp tension changes, giving rise to variations in the pattern.

After a short length of carpet has been knotted, and each row of knots packed down with a comb or knife, the weaver trims it with a large pair of shearing scissors. The image of the design is then clearly revealed. Finally, once the carpet is complete, it is washed to remove the stiffness and to restore the luster to the rug.

Aside from being floor coverings, carpets are used as furnishing fabrics, drapes, wall hangings and animal saddlebags. Perhaps one of the most famous carpets ever made was a Persian kilim carpet known as the "Spring of Khosru." Like the first carpet Vachagan weaves for Anaeet, it depicted a garden — inspired by the Islamic notion that paradise takes the form of a garden. It was over 200 feet long and, like the second carpet in the story, was made from gold and silver thread, as well as silk and precious and semiprecious stones. Running streams were marked by crystal, the ground woven in golden thread, the leaves worked in silk, and blossom represented by precious stones. It was indeed a magic carpet!

Clever Anaeet
Armenian

Once in the land of Armenia a fine young prince called Vachagan was born. As he grew up, he learned all the courtly arts — languages, music and poetry — but his favorite pastime was hunting.

One spring morning when Vachagan was out hunting, he came across a small village. He had been riding for hours under the hot sun. His mouth was parched and his head was swimming. Around the well stood a group of girls filling their buckets with cool, fresh water. Seeing how hot Vachagan looked, one of them lifted a pitcher of water to him. Vachagan was about to drink from it when another girl snatched the pitcher from him and poured the water back into her own bucket. Vachagan stared as the girl refilled the pitcher and poured it back into her bucket again. This she repeated several times, as if to tease him, then finally lifted the pitcher and offered it to him. Vachagan gulped down the water, then looked up. "Is it the custom here to tease strangers?" he asked.

"I did not mean to tease you," answered the young girl. "You were very hot and it would have harmed you to drink the cold water. You needed to cool down a little first."

The girl's reply impressed Vachagan, as did her beauty. "What is your name?" he asked.

"I am Anaeet, daughter of Aran the shepherd," she replied. "Who are you?"

Vachagan smiled. "I cannot tell you now but you will learn soon enough."

With that, Vachagan returned to the palace where he announced that he wished to marry Anaeet, the shepherd's daughter.

His mother protested. "Vachagan, many princesses are worthy of your attention. A prince should not marry a shepherdess."

But Vachagan was determined. Finally his parents agreed to send a messenger to Anaeet's village with gifts and an offer of marriage.

Aran the shepherd welcomed the royal messenger and laid a carpet down before him. Upon this the messenger placed fine cloths, jewels and precious oils. When he introduced himself, Anaeet smiled. So the handsome stranger was Prince Vachagan, she thought to herself. But when the messenger asked for Anaeet's hand in marriage on behalf of the prince, she frowned. "Tell me," she asked, "what is the prince's trade?"

The messenger looked aghast. "He is the prince; he has no need of a trade, for all the king's subjects are his servants."

"Prince one day, pauper the next," replied Anaeet. "Everyone should have a trade for no one knows the twisting of fate. I will not marry a man without a trade."

The messenger carried Anaeet's reply to the palace, where the queen and king secretly breathed a sigh of relief. But Vachagan was not discouraged.

"Anaeet's council is wise," he said. "Of course all men should have a trade." And he summoned the royal advisors to help him choose a profession.

After much discussion, it was decided that weaving would be the most suitable trade for a prince. A craftsman from the royal workshop was assigned as his tutor. Within the cycle of seasons, Vachagan had mastered his craft.

Vachagan wove for Anaeet a beautiful carpet depicting a garden. Then he summoned a royal messenger to carry the carpet to the home of Aran the shepherd. Anaeet smiled when she was presented with the carpet, and willingly agreed to their marriage.

So Vachagan and Anaeet were wed. The festivities lasted seven days and seven nights. There was music and dancing, and the tables fairly groaned under the weight of all the food.

The young couple lived happily together. And when the old king and queen died, Vachagan was crowned king. In the years that followed there was much rejoicing, for never had the people of Armenia been ruled so justly.

However, as the years passed, a strange thing began to occur. People would come to the palace and report their friends and relatives missing. Mothers told of sons who had not returned from the marketplace, wives told of husbands who had disappeared. As the number of reports grew, so did the concern of the king and queen.

"It is strange," said Anaeet, "that so many people should disappear. Perhaps you should ride out among our people and see for yourself."

And so, dressed as a peasant, Vachagan set out, leaving clever Anaeet to rule in his place. He sat by village wells and listened to the gossip and walked unrecognized among his wealthiest and poorest subjects alike. Everywhere he went, he heard stories of missing people, but still he was no closer to solving the mystery.

One day he came to a busy town. There, in the marketplace, he caught sight of a crowd of men. Moving closer, Vachagan saw that they were hovering around a man dressed as a priest. He was singing, and to one side of him sat another priest. The man's voice was clear and sweet. It had a strangely hypnotic quality about it, and the men encircling him seemed oddly silent. The singer and his fellow priest turned and began to walk toward the town gates. As if in a trance, the crowd followed him and Vachagan accompanied them.

From the gates they processed out into the countryside and toward the hills. There they reached a high stone wall in which there stood a great heavy wooden door. The first priest took a large key from the folds of his cloak and unlocked the door.

Inside the door was a huge square. On one side of it stood a great temple whose stone shone red in the sun; on another side stood a smaller temple. Vachagan and the other men were led to this temple, which concealed the entrance to a cavern. One by one, the men filed through the doorway. Behind them, the iron door groaned shut. Darkness closed about them and Vachagan and his companions stumbled blindly forward. The air was cold and dank.

As their eyes adjusted to the gloom, they saw a thin and bent figure hobbling toward them. "Follow me," he rasped, barely lifting a bony, gnarled hand to show them the way.

They were led through three huge caverns filled with men in as pitiful a state as their own guide. Each of them toiled at a trade, some stitching, others carving or knitting.

"Alas," gasped their guide, "that evil priest has led you too to your doom. For everyone who is brought to this place must surely die, though some more quickly than others. All those with trades work until they die, while those without are put to death immediately."

At that moment, a priest approached, escorted by armed guards. He pushed the guide roughly to one side and addressed the men.

"Which of you here has a trade?"

Vachagan stepped boldly forward and spoke: "We all do, for we can

weave carpets the like of which you will have never seen before. They are more valuable than gold and as fine as the down on a bird's breast."

The priest's eyes narrowed as he gave orders for the necessary materials to be brought. "If your boast proves to be untrue, then you will all be skinned alive," he snarled.

At once the team were set to work and Vachagan instructed them. The men's backs were bent hour after hour over the loom as their shuttles flew back and forth. Their eyes ached from following the fine pattern in the gloom, their skin paled and they grew thin and gaunt. But slowly, under the guidance of Vachagan, the most beautiful carpet began to emerge. Its richly colored threads were woven into intricate patterns, while gold thread formed sacred symbols and signs of good fortune. And embroidered into the complex tapestry was a message. It told of Vachagan's imprisonment and his whereabouts, but it was visible only to the most discerning eye.

Finally the carpet was completed. The priest was indeed impressed.

"This carpet is fit for royalty," Vachagan hinted, "for there are ancient signs and symbols woven into the cloth that would not be understood by common folk. And I am sure that even Queen Anaeet would marvel at its beauty. I warrant she would pay you handsomely for it."

That very night, the priest set off for the palace.

Queen Anaeet had ruled wisely in Vachagan's absence. But now, as the year was drawing to a close, she worried for her husband's safety. Whenever merchants, minstrels and other travelers visited the palace, she listened closely to their stories, hoping for news of Vachagan.

One morning, as Queen Anaeet sat in the palace garden, a servant announced the arrival of a priest.

"Your Majesty," the servant said, "this visitor boasts of a woven carpet fit only for the eyes of a queen."

When the priest was admitted, he bowed and proceeded to unroll the carpet with a flourish. Anaeet's attendants gasped with amazement as the light caught the golden threads of the carpet.

But Queen Anaeet gave the carpet hardly a second look. Her heart was heavy and she was constantly distracted now by the fear that some misfortune had befallen her husband. The priest, sensing her lack of interest, began to praise every detail of the carpet. "Your Majesty, there is no other carpet like this one. It outshines the stars and is more delicate to the touch than the petals of a rose. But what is more, O Majesty, it is endowed with magical properties. It has signs and symbols that may be understood only by one as wise as yourself."

Anaeet's attention was caught at last. Holding a corner of the carpet in her hands, she saw letters woven cleverly into the design. She read the message with growing excitement, realizing that it came from Vachagan. It explained that the bearer of the carpet was his jailer; it described the terrible suffering of the king and his companions; and it gave the whereabouts of their prison.

Quickly Anaeet ordered the priest to be seized and the army to be summoned. She herself rode at their head and led them from the palace.

They rode for some time, closely following Vachagan's directions. At last, Anaeet saw ahead of them the top of the red stone temple. Mistaking the clamoring of Anaeet's army for the sound of more prisoners arriving, the priests unlocked the gates and the army rode straight in.

Within minutes, the royal soldiers had captured all the priests and forced open the great iron door that led to the secret caverns. Out stumbled the prisoners, blinded by the bright sunlight and near to death from the ill-treatment they had suffered. Last of all came Vachagan, carrying in his arms a man too weak to walk.

Anaeet and Vachagan embraced, tears falling from their eyes in their joy at seeing each other again. Freed at last from their living hell, the men threw themselves at Queen Anaeet's feet, crying, "One thousand blessings to Queen Anaeet, who has saved our lives today!"

As the cheers grew fainter, Vachagan spoke: "My friends, it is not once but twice that our queen has saved us. For, many years ago, she insisted that all men should have a trade, even a king's son. Praise be to her for her wisdom, for without it we would all have surely perished."

As the weeks passed, the news of Vachagan's adventures spread throughout the kingdom, and the wisdom of the beautiful Queen Anaeet was celebrated in story and song. And while not a thread remains of the beautiful carpet that Vachagan once wove with the aid of his fellow captives, we still have — for as long as tongue is willing to tell and ear to listen — the golden thread of his story.

Fabrics of East Africa

The cloth in this story is a magical one. It is described as soft yet very strong, able to keep the wearer both warm and cool. And although it is very long, it can be folded up into a tiny bundle.

The "earthly" cloth that this most resembles is silk, but silk was not traditionally woven in the Swahili-speaking region of East Africa where this story comes from. Here, cloth was traditionally woven from locally grown and hand-spun cotton, and the fabric in the story also has some of the qualities of very fine cotton lawn. Moving further inland, fibers prepared from the leaves of the raffia plant are also woven into cloth. The women of the Kuba people, for instance, embroider dyed and woven raffia cloth. The Kuba also stitch glass beads onto cloth to create royal regalia and other ceremonial objects.

In many African countries, all weaving is done by men. In areas where both men and women weave, each sex usually has a different type of loom. Once it has been woven, the cloth is dyed with colors from local vegetable and mineral sources — indigo is the most common.

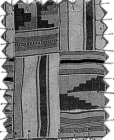

In East Africa, nonwoven fabrics are also widespread. For instance, the Masai women of Kenya stitch beads onto animal

18

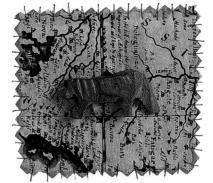

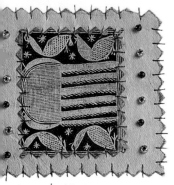

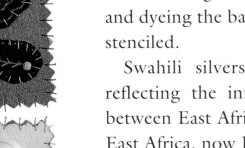

hide clothing. And in Uganda, bark cloth is made by felting and dyeing the barks of certain trees, which are then painted or stenciled.

Swahili silversmithing and metalworking is renowned, reflecting the influence of over a thousand years of trade between East Africa and Arabia and India. Part of the coast of East Africa, now Kenya, was settled by the Arabs as early as the eighth century AD. So it is interesting that the main character in this story, Fatima (who herself bears an Arab name), always appears bedecked in jewels and precious metals. She also wears the intricate beadwork and coiled-wire jewelry that are typical of this area.

Fatima dresses in rich cloth and fine silks, which her husband, as a merchant, would have been able to obtain for her. Clearly, though, the serpent's cloth is something much more special than any fabric he could buy. Its properties link it to a tradition of clothing with magical properties (a cloak of invisibility, for instance, or a pair of enchanted shoes that can transport the hero anywhere in a trice). It is not described in terms of color — all we are told is that it is patterned and shimmers and shines in the dark. But the association with gold, and the life-and-death battle needed to win it, all add to its otherworldliness.

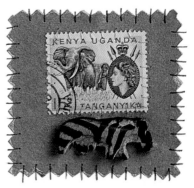

The Cloth of the Serpent Pembe Mirui

Swahili

*O*nce in a small village there lived a young woman called Fatima, who was married to Amadi the merchant. Amadi loved his wife more than anything else in the world, and there was nothing he would refuse her. As he went about his work trading and selling his wares, he would think about returning to the village in the evening and being greeted by Fatima's warm, welcoming smile.

Amadi was a happy man. And there was nothing he liked more than to lavish gifts upon Fatima — fine silks, intricate beadwork, jewels, gold and silver. "Beauty for my beauty," he would say.

Soon the other women in the village grew jealous of Fatima. They looked at her fine clothes and her golden bracelets, and their lips would draw tight. They would sneer at her jewels and say, "Fatima, that gold is of poor quality and those jewels are only glass. That cloth that you wear, it is nothing compared to the cloth of the serpent Pembe Mirui."

"What is the cloth of the serpent Pembe Mirui?" asked Fatima.

"The cloth of the serpent Pembe Mirui? Why, it is the most beautiful cloth in all the world. It is so finely woven, the design so intricate, and the colors so brilliant and alluring. If your husband truly loved you, he would fetch you this — the rarest fabric a woman could have."

At first Fatima ignored the other women's whispering, but each day they spoke the same poisonous words, until her poor heart was filled with sadness and a longing for the fine cloth.

Amadi noticed Fatima's sadness.

"Fatima, why is it that you look so gloomy?" he asked.

"Aah, Amadi, you have given me many fine presents. But I can only be sure of your love if you fetch me the cloth of the serpent Pembe Mirui."

"Fatima, I do not know where to start searching for such a thing. Nevertheless, to assure you of my love, I shall find it for you."

That very evening, Amadi prepared for his journey. He took food and counted fifty rupees into his belt. Early the next morning, just as the sun was creeping over the horizon, he set out. He walked from village to village and city to city. In the crowded marketplaces and on the dusty streets he would ask the whereabouts of the cloth of the serpent Pembe Mirui. But, each time, the people he asked would simply shake their heads and turn away.

Amadi's heart grew heavy and he began to imagine that he would never find the cloth of the serpent Pembe Mirui. Then one day he came upon a poor old woman sitting on the step of a small hut. She was stooped over with age, her wrinkled, bony hands clasped together on her lap.

"Good morning, old woman," greeted Amadi.

"Good morning," replied the old woman. "Could you spare a coin for an old woman on your way to market?"

"Aah, Mother," sighed Amadi, squatting down beside the old woman. "If only I was going to the market; that would be an easy thing. But my journey is longer than that." He handed the old woman a coin from his belt.

"Tell me about your journey," said the old woman, fingering the shiny coin.

"I am looking for the cloth of the serpent Pembe Mirui to present to my beloved wife," Amadi replied.

The old woman gave a crooked smile. "The cloth of the serpent Pembe Mirui? I could help you there." She gave a clap and from the hut came a sleek black cat, walking on its hind legs and carrying a bag under its arm.

The old woman turned to the cat. "See this man," she said. "He needs the cloth of the serpent Pembe Mirui. You must show him the way and be his traveling companion."

Amadi stared at the cat. The cat straightened its whiskers and gave a nod to the old woman.

"Remember," said the old woman, turning to Amadi, "whatever you ask, ask three times."

Amadi thanked the old woman for her advice and set off down the road. The sleek black cat trotted alongside him. At each crossroad they reached, the cat would give a swing of its tail and lead Amadi ever onward.

It wasn't long before Amadi and the cat came upon a huge serpent, its body stretched across the road. The serpent was asleep. Dark scales rippled up and down its body as the sleeping breath passed with a loud purr through its cavernous hairy nostrils.

Amadi's heart was pounding with fear. He stepped forward and, with a quaver in his voice, addressed the sleeping serpent in almost a whisper: "Are you the serpent Pembe Mirui?"

Another great breath rippled along the serpent's body, but the creature made no response. Amadi looked anxiously towards the cat, then he remembered the words of the old woman: "Whatever you ask, ask three times." Amadi repeated his question twice more, each time a little louder: "Are you the serpent Pembe Mirui?" And as he spoke for the third time, one of the huge scaly eyelids lifted and a bright orange eye fixed upon him.

The serpent replied three times, "No, I am not Pembe Mirui."

Although very frightened, Amadi felt his heart sink. But the sleek black cat just gave a swing of its tail and continued along the road. So Amadi followed.

A little further on, they came across a tall, spreading tree. Its branches were bare, and curled about its trunk was a two-headed gray serpent with two thickly spiked tails. Again Amadi approached the serpent and asked three times, "Are you the serpent Pembe Mirui?"

And again the serpent replied three times, "No, I am not Pembe Mirui."

On the banks of a great river, Amadi and the cat found a three-headed red serpent whose voice crackled and spat, but neither was this the serpent Pembe Mirui.

Basking in the hot sun, coiled about a large rock, was a four-headed orange serpent, whose heads replied in unison, "No, I am not Pembe Mirui."

Nor was the five-headed yellow serpent that lay in a great nest of bones and feathers.

Three times Amadi chanted to the blue six-headed serpent the question "Are you the serpent Pembe Mirui?" Although the serpent was larger and more hideous than the previous five, it shook its six heads: "No, I am not Pembe Mirui."

Amadi hung his head. The day was drawing to a close and his feet felt as heavy as large river stones wedged in the mud. Pointing to a thicket of trees, Amadi called to the cat, "Let us rest here tonight."

As Amadi and the cat entered the sunless thicket, ahead of them they saw an enormous golden serpent with seven heads. Its seven tails were coiled into seven spirals and its body glowed like the sun itself. Amadi placed his hand on his sword and called out three times: "Tell me, serpent, are you Pembe Mirui?" The great monster lifted up its seven heads and all fourteen eyes bored down upon Amadi as it boomed in reply, "I am Pembe Mirui!"

The ground beneath Amadi shook as the serpent arched its body. The seven tails snapped straight and the seven heads swooped and dived.

The sleek black cat called to Amadi, who stood there trembling, "Do not move, Amadi, or it will strike you. Be on your guard."

Amadi stood silent and still as a statue. The serpent reared up on its seven tails and lunged down upon Amadi, hissing and spraying poisonous venom. Amadi leaped to one side, pulled his sword from his belt and, with a rapid swing, sliced cleanly through one of the serpent's heads. The serpent recoiled with a scream that brought the birds down dead from the sky.

The sleek black cat sprang forward and, dodging between the pools of venom that lay on the ground, snatched up the serpent's lost head and placed it in the bag. Again Pembe Mirui swept down to attack, its twelve remaining eyes blazing with pain and anger.

Again Amadi swung his sword bravely and two more of the mighty serpent's heads rolled to the ground.

The battle continued, the serpent writhing with fury and intent on destroying Amadi. But with each attack, another of the serpent's heads was sliced from its body and the cat would nimbly dodge between the sword and the serpent and retrieve the fallen heads for its bag.

Only one of Pembe Mirui's heads now remained. As Amadi raised his sword one last time and brought it down with an almighty swing, the serpent spat from its mouth a shower of poisonous venom. Amadi leaped out of the way and the final golden head fell harmlessly to the ground.

Amadi ran over to where the dead body of Pembe Mirui lay. Reaching inside the serpent's skin, he searched with his hand and pulled out the most exquisite fabric. It shimmered and shone in the dark of the thicket.

The woven patterns seemed to ripple through it like water. It was as soft and as smooth as the skin of a newborn child. Yet, despite its softness, the fabric showed no sign of weakness when Amadi pulled it.

Amadi wrapped the cloth about him. It covered him from head to foot and had the remarkable effect of keeping him both warm and cool at the same time. When he folded it, it would fit snugly into the palm of his hand. Indeed it was the most remarkable cloth that Amadi had ever seen. He carefully tucked it into his pocket and turned to face the cat, who was standing waiting for him with its bag under one arm.

Amadi followed the sleek black cat along the road and soon they were standing once again outside the old woman's hut. The cat handed the old woman the bag containing the seven heads of Pembe Mirui, and Amadi handed her the coin belt containing the remaining rupees.

Amadi thanked the old woman and the cat, but just as he was about to leave, the old woman took his hand and said, "Amadi, it is not every day that a man's love should be so tested. Tell your wife to be content. A foolish whim of hers nearly cost her husband's life; and what strength is there in a dead man's love?"

When Amadi reached home, Fatima greeted him joyously. Amadi placed the cloth of Pembe Mirui into her hands. Fatima was overcome with the beauty of the fabric. She wrapped it about her body and paraded around the house. But when she heard Amadi's tale of the seven-headed serpent, of the dangers he had faced, and the wise words of the old woman, she felt heartily ashamed of her own doubt.

"Husband, I know the wonder of this cloth is matched by the strength of your love for me. I shall never doubt it again."

And from that day forth and for many years to come, Fatima and Amadi lived happily in the knowledge of each other's abiding love.

The Story of Silk

$\mathcal{L}egend$ has it that silk was first made in China nearly five thousand years ago. Its production remained a closely guarded secret until the Chinese merchants started to carry silk to India and the Middle East. The celebrated Silk Road, along which silk was transported from China to the West, flourished from ancient until medieval times.

From about the eighth century, silk production spread to Europe and between the twelfth and seventeenth centuries, important weaving centers were established in Spain, Italy, France, and England.

In China, silk was so highly valued that it was used as a form of currency in its own right. It also enjoyed a special religious status and a grand ceremony was held every year to worship the chief goddess of silk, Lei Tsu. To show her respect for the goddess, the empress herself took care of a silkworm house, just as the farmers' wives did.

The maker of silk is a very humble caterpillar, the larva of the silk moth, or *Bombyx mori*. The larvae feed on mulberry leaves for six to eight weeks, at which point they turn from an apple-green color to a soft creamy white and begin to spin themselves a "little silk house," or chrysalis. Inside the

chrysalis, the silkworm waves its head in a continual figure of eight, depositing layer upon layer of silk thread. At this stage, the chrysalis is either plunged into hot water or held in scalding steam to prevent the moth from leaving the cocoon and destroying the silk.

Two winding processes are used to make the silk thread. The first is "reeling" — the unwinding of the cocoons. Several cocoons are unwound simultaneously, each producing 2,000-3,000 feet of silk thread. The silk is then washed, threaded through an eyelet, and spun on to a reel.

The second winding process is called "throwing." Here, several silk threads are twisted together to form a stronger yarn. The tightness of this twist gives varying qualities of yarn. The silk is also boiled in soap to remove the natural gum, then bleached or dyed. Once the thread has been prepared, it can be used to make different types of silk fabrics, such as brocade, damask, velvet, and satin.

The silk textile in this story is brocade. Brocading is the process by which a raised design in a satin or twill weave is added to the fabric when it is being woven. As the story shows, hand embroidery can also be incorporated into the woven design. Brocading is often confused with embroidery and tapestry. However, it is a form of fabric manufacture in its own right.

The Silk Brocade
Chinese

Long ago, there lived an old widow and her three sons. They led a modest life, and each member of the family worked hard. The sons tended a small vegetable patch and took odd jobs, while their mother collected firewood and wove silk. The old woman was famous for her skill in weaving brocade. Her work was so fine and detailed, the colors so bright and well chosen and the scenes she wove so lifelike, that she had hardly finished one brocade when it would be sold and she would start on the next.

One day, as she made her way to the marketplace to sell one of her brocades, the old woman passed by a small shop. Inside the shop, she caught sight of the most enchanting picture she had ever seen. It depicted a grand house set in a beautiful garden, with fruit trees and beds of brightly colored flowers. There was a small fishpond and a vegetable plot, with chickens and ducks pecking the ground. As the old woman looked at the picture, she felt a great sense of peace settle on her.

That night, as the family sat eating their meal, the old woman told her sons of the beautiful picture she had seen.

"Imagine living in a place like that," she sighed. "How happy I would be!"

The two older sons smiled. "Perhaps, Mother, when we die, we shall be reborn in such a place."

But the youngest son felt only joy at seeing his mother so happy. "Mother, why don't you weave the picture yourself?" he said. "Then you would have it always to look upon."

In her excitement, the old woman rushed at once to her loom and began to weave the picture that she had seen. And as the shuttle passed to and fro, so did the days. The days became weeks, the weeks became months, and the seasons turned, but still the old woman sat and still she wove.

The eldest sons began to complain that she had not made any brocade for the market for months. But the youngest son defended his mother. "Let her be," he said. "Can't you see how important that picture is to her? She has been a good mother to us all. Don't begrudge her this."

Slowly, under the skillful hand of the old woman, a picture began to take shape in the brocade. In the first year, tears fell from the old woman's eyes on to the brocade, forming a crystal-clear pool where golden fish swam and lotus flowers tripped across the surface. In the second year, a gray hair from her head formed a wisp of smoke that curled from the chimney on the tiled roof of the grand house. And in the third year, drops of blood fell from her hard-worn fingers and formed a brilliant red sun that shone down upon the trees, upon the rice fields that seemed to sway in a breeze and upon the beds of nodding flowers, so lifelike you could almost smell them.

Finally the brocade was finished. It was so detailed and beautifully woven that it seemed like a doorway framing the entrance to another world.

The three sons carried the brocade to an open window so that they could admire the colors in the sunlight, when, all of a sudden, a gust of wind snatched the cloth from their hands and whipped it out of the window and into the sky, where it disappeared from sight. The old woman dashed outside and stared hopelessly into the sky. Her sons rushed to comfort her. But the old woman could say nothing: her eyes glazed over with tears.

"Come inside, Mother," called the older sons as the stars began to sprinkle the night sky and the air became crisp and cold. But the old woman just stood and continued to stare upward, the tears rolling down her face.

"Mother, we will find the brocade for you," promised the youngest son, and, taking his mother's hand in his, he led her inside.

But the old woman would not eat or drink, and there was nothing that her sons could say or do that would comfort her. Finally the eldest son declared, "I will go forth, Mother, and bring back your brocade."

The son passed through many towns and villages and at each of them inquired about the brocade, but no one had seen such a wondrous thing as he described. After many days, he reached the foot of a huge mountain, where he found a small cave. At the mouth of the cave grew a tree laden with red berries. A stone horse stood under the tree, and beside the horse sat a toothless, white-haired old woman. "What brings you here, my son?"

"I am looking for my mother's brocade," he replied. "It is the most beautiful piece of cloth and took three years to weave. But a strange wind arose and snatched it from us, and now I am trying to find it."

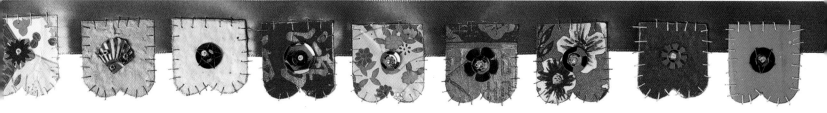

The old woman grinned. "I know the brocade of which you speak. It was so beautiful that it caught the attention of the maidens of the Sun Mountain that lies to the east. They have stolen it for themselves."

"I must ask them to return it," said the son. "Please tell me if you know how I may reach the Sun Mountain."

"Ah," said the old woman. "It is a difficult journey. First you must knock out your two front teeth and place them in the mouth of my stone horse. After the horse has eaten red berries from the tree, you must climb on its back. Your way to the Sun Mountain lies through a valley of fire, where the flames will roar and crackle about you, but you must show no fear or you will be burned to a cinder. You will then reach a wide, wild sea, where the waves will tower above you and the wind's breath will strike through you like a dagger of ice. You must not cry out or the ocean will swallow you up. Once you have crossed this ocean, you will reach the Sun Mountain."

When he heard the old woman's words, the eldest son shivered.

"My son, I see that you are afraid. Such a journey is clearly not for you," said the old woman. "Why don't you take this gift from me instead?" And she gave the young man a fat pouch of gold.

33

The eldest son accepted her gift but he never returned to his mother. With his pockets lined with gold, he headed south, thinking fortune would follow him.

Months passed and the eldest son did not return. Seeing his mother still so pale and silent, the second son stood up and announced: "Some misfortune must have befallen my brother. I will go forth and find your brocade for you, Mother." And he, too, set off toward the east.

Again, fate led him to the foot of the huge mountain, where the toothless, white-haired old woman sat with her stone horse. And when she spoke of the valley of fire and the cruel and icy ocean, he, too, shuddered and accepted instead her gift of gold. Ashamed of his fear, he, too, chose a path that led away from his home.

By now the old widow woman had taken to her bed. Her eyes, lacking hope, had grown dull and her skin looked gray. It broke the youngest son's heart to see his mother so unhappy and ill.

"Mother, let me go and look for your brocade. I would rather search this world over than to see you so unhappy."

With that, the youngest son kissed his mother goodbye and set off in the direction he had watched his brothers take. Finally he reached the foot of the huge mountain, where the old woman sat.

"Ah, your two brothers passed this way," she said. "And they each left with a pouch of gold. You may have one too if, like them, you cannot face the journey to find the brocade."

"Gold would be a poor price for my mother's brocade," replied the boy. "Besides, I fear that if I do not return with it soon, then she will die. And what use is gold to the dead?"

So again the old woman repeated her instructions. At once the boy picked up a stone and knocked out his two front teeth. He placed them in the mouth of the stone horse, who tossed her mane and ate the red berries. The boy climbed on her back and the horse sprang forward.

Through the valley of fire they passed, and though the flames licked about the boy and his skin and hair were scorched, not a flicker of fear showed on his face. Over the cruel, churning ocean they galloped, where the waves towered high and thundered about them and the wind whipped the youth's skin raw with its sharp, icy breath. But he neither shuddered nor cried out. Then, looming ahead of them, he saw the Sun Mountain at last, rising golden and glowing on the far shore.

On the slopes of the Sun Mountain lay a grand palace. As the horse drew nearer, the youngest son thought he could hear tinkling laughter and musical voices. He dismounted and stepped inside the palace, where his eyes fell at once upon a group of sun maidens. They were the most beautiful women that he had ever seen. Like shafts of light they danced about the hall, their gentle laughter echoing sweetly.

Then he saw something hanging on the far wall that caused a wave of joy to sweep over him. It was none other than his old mother's brocade!

"I have come to fetch the brocade," he explained to the sun maidens, who were surprised by the boy's sudden appearance. "It belongs to my mother from whom it was stolen. At this very moment she lies wrapped in a grief

that eats away at her for the loss of her brocade. Once it brought her such joy, but now, without it, she will surely die."

"You may return the brocade to your mother very soon for our work is almost completed," said one of the maidens. "We never meant to keep the brocade, only to copy it. We, too, were spellbound by its beauty."

The youngest son looked about the room again and noticed for the first time a silver loom standing in the middle of the hall. On it was stretched a copy of his mother's brocade.

"If you will spend this evening with us, tomorrow we shall return the brocade," continued the maiden.

The sun maidens ushered the youngest son to a table at one end of the hall. Sweet fruit and cool wine were brought to him. He was hungry and ate quickly. The wine made his head heavy and soon he fell into a deep sleep.

While the boy slept, the maidens continued to work on into the night. A large pearl hung from the ceiling and they worked by its pale glow.

One maiden worked more quickly than the others. She completed her part of the brocade and stood back to admire it. But as her eye moved from the copy to the original brocade, her heart sank. For it was clear that the old woman's handiwork was far superior.

36

How wonderful it would be if she could live in a place like the one in the brocade, the maiden thought to herself. Picking up a needle and thread, she quietly approached the old woman's brocade. Then, while no one was looking, she embroidered a figure standing by the pond — a girl just like her, with a bright pink dress and long black hair.

Much later that night, the youngest son awoke. He was surprised to find the hall empty. But there, by the light of the pearl, he could see his mother's brocade and not far from it the uncompleted work of the sun maidens.

The boy walked over to his mother's brocade. He stood there running his fingers over the silky fabric. He thought of his poor, ill mother and how pale and frail she had looked when he had last seen her. Fearing that she might die before he returned with her precious brocade, he suddenly snatched up the cloth and ran from the hall. The horse was waiting for him patiently outside. In the dark of the night, the two of them stole quickly away.

Back across the icy ocean and the valley of fire they flew until they were once again standing outside the cave at the bottom of the mountain.

They were greeted by the old woman. She reached up and helped the youngest son dismount from the horse. Then, taking from the horse its two front teeth, she replaced them in the boy's mouth. Instantly the horse turned back into stone. Finally she presented the youngest son with a pair of deerskin moccasins, wished him well and sent him on his way.

Before he knew it, the magic shoes had whisked the boy straight to his own front door. He ran into the house and up to his mother's bed. "Mother," he whispered, holding her hand. "Mother, I have your brocade."

The old woman's eyes slowly opened and in them the boy caught a glimmer of joy. He placed the fabric in her hand. "Here, Mother, let me carry you into the sunlight so that you may see it better," he said as he lifted her gently and carried her through the door.

Outside, he carefully laid his mother down and held up the brocade for her to see. But as he did so a wind suddenly caught the cloth, but gently this time. Instead of blowing away, the fabric merely billowed and grew. It doubled, it tripled in size. It wrapped itself around the youth and the old woman and, lo and behold, the two of them found themselves standing in the most beautiful garden. All around them were fruit trees, richly laden, and flowers grew like a carpet beneath their feet. There in the distance was a beautiful house and standing near the pool was a young woman.

"Greetings," she said, her voice like shimmering silver. "I am one of the sun maidens. Forgive me, but I so loved your fine work and this beautiful place you have created that I knew I could not be happy unless I lived here myself. Please may I stay with you in this fine house and garden?"

The mother and her son agreed at once. Now that her brocade had been returned to her, it wasn't long before the old woman became well again. Nor was it very long before the youngest son and the sun maiden were married. All three of them lived contentedly in their woven paradise.

One day two beggars passed by, the scruffiest sight you ever did see. They were none other than the two older brothers, fallen on hard times. But when they looked in at the garden and saw their brother and his beautiful wife and their mother, her eyes bright with happiness, they felt so ashamed that they slunk quietly away, never to return.

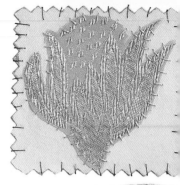

Fabrics from the Pacific Islands

The three textiles in this story are tapa (bark cloth), ulana (woven matting) and the ceremonial feather cape or cloak. The first two items are found throughout the South Pacific, but feather cloaks are unique to Hawaii and New Zealand. All three textiles are made by women and all of them are highly prized items.

Tapa cloth can be made from the bark of several different trees. The most common are the paper mulberry, wake and mamaki. The bark is stripped from the tree trunk and left to soak in water for several days. This makes it easy to separate the coarse outer bark from the soft inner fiber. The fiber is then pounded into a pulp with wooden mallets that are carved with distinctive patterns. The pulp is beaten into strips and left to dry. Several tapa strips are then joined together to form the cloth. Sometimes fragrant flowers are pounded or sewn into the cloth to create a lasting fragrance.

Tapa cloth is often dyed using colors from plants and sea animals. The colors range from gray to purple, pink and red. The dyes are applied either by being painted on by hand or by using wooden block prints.

The principal use for tapa cloth was as clothing. Like silk, it had considerable value and was often traded, offered as a gift — in this story, Eleio presents it as a gift to his chief — or used in ceremonies.

The ulana, or woven mat, is used as floor covering and as furnishing. High-quality mats also had a ceremonial use and were worn as clothing. The most commonly used plant for making ulana is the lau nala (pandanus plant). The preparation of leaves from this plant involves a lengthy process of stripping, soaking, drying and heating before weaving can begin.

The feather cape is a highly prized item that is passed down through generations as a way of bestowing power and status. Traditionally, such cloaks are worn only by men.

To make a cape, feathers, collected from native birds such as the i'iwi, mamo, apapane and the o'o, are fastened to a net of cord woven from fibers of the South Pacific flax plant. Yellow and red feathers are the most highly prized.

Both tapa cloth and feathers were once a form of currency among the islanders of the South Pacific. For instance, professional bird hunters paid their taxes to the ali'i (chieftain) in the form of feathers. Captain Cook, in a visit to Tahiti in 1777, observed tufts of red feathers being used by priests during a human sacrifice. He always made sure he had a supply of red feathers with him to trade with the islanders.

The Feather Cloak
Hawaiian

Far away, across the oceans of the South Pacific, lies the island of Maui. Had you the view of a seafaring bird, you could see that the island of Maui is the shape of a man's torso and head, bent at the waist, looking out across the waters toward the neighboring island of Kahoolawe.

On the island of Maui there once lived a man by the name of Eleio. Now Eleio was a special man in many ways. His fleetness of foot had earned him the title of Kukini, which means "trained runner." Eleio was a "tohunga" — he could see into the secret world of the spirits. He had the gift of healing, he knew how to prepare medicines from plants, and it was also said that he had the power to bring the dead back to life.

Now, as you can imagine, Eleio was a very useful person to have about. As it happened, Eleio worked in the service of Kakaalaneo, chief of Maui. One day the chief called Eleio to him and said, "Eleio, I want you to fetch me a kava root from Hana for a special celebration this evening."

Although Hana lay on the other side of the island, Kakaalaneo knew that Eleio was the swiftest and most reliable of his runners and expected him to return with the root within hours.

Eleio began to make his way across the island through the quivering thick green forest. All of a sudden, he caught sight of a young woman up ahead of him. It was not unusual to see other people here in the forest, but this woman was of exceptional beauty. Her long black hair hung down her back and her face was as fresh and as radiant as the moon. She looked at Eleio from over her shoulder and then darted away into the forest.

Eleio was curious, and instead of continuing onward to Hana, he veered off the path to follow her. After all, he was the swiftest Kukini in the chief of Maui's service and it would take but a few minutes to catch up with the woman and ask her name.

Eleio hastened his steps. Again he caught sight of the woman. She waved to him. Eleio sprang forward, but try as he might he was unable to catch up with her, no matter how fast he ran. She dodged nimbly through the forest, over rocks, hills, mountains, through deep valleys and along winding streams until at last they came to the Cape of Hana-manu-loa. Here she stopped outside a poua, a tower-like building made of bamboo.

Eleio knew this tower to be a special place of the dead — the funeral house of chieftains, their families and other distinguished people. It was here that their bodies were laid out, exposed to the elements — the sea, air and sun.

The woman turned to Eleio and cried out, "Eleio, swiftest Kukini and skilled tohunga, I am Kanikani-aula. I am no longer of this world, Eleio. I am a spirit and this tower is where I dwell for now."

"Aah," smiled Eleio, "that is why I could not catch you. Only a spirit could move so quickly."

Kanikani-aula smiled back at him. "Yes, I led you on a wild chase, Eleio. But now let us be friends for it is lonely for me here in this poua."

For a time Kanikani-aula and Eleio sat and spoke together. Then Kanikani-aula stood and pointed back to where they had run from. "Not far from here live my family. Go to them now, Eleio, and ask them for a hog, rolls of tapa cloth, fine woven mats and the feather cloak I was making.

The cloak is not finished but there are enough feathers and netting in the whare, our home, to finish it. Bring them here and I will complete the cloak for you and give you these gifts as a token of our friendship." With these words, Kanikani-aula disappeared from sight.

Eleio climbed up into the poua and there, lying on a platform halfway up the tower, he saw the dead body of Kanikani-aula. She was in every way as lovely as the spirit. She lay there beautifully dressed, with a look of peace on her face. Eleio could tell that she had not been dead for long.

Leaving the poua, he ran in the direction that Kanikani-aula had pointed. There he came across an older woman who stood weeping. Eleio guessed that this must be her mother.

"Aloha," he greeted the woman. "My name is Eleio, Kukini and tohunga of Kakaalaneo, chief of Maui. I am a stranger to these parts but I was led here by the spirit of Kanikani-aula."

The older woman stopped weeping as Eleio described the spirit woman and explained Kanikani-aula's request. Quickly she ran and fetched her husband and Eleio repeated his story. The man and the woman willingly agreed to give Eleio the tapa cloth, the mats and the feather cloak, but as they began discussing the hog, Eleio had an idea.

"Tell me," he said to Kanikani-aula's father, "are all these people who live about you your friends?"

"Why, yes," answered the man. "They are cousins, aunts, uncles, brothers, sisters and friends of Kanikani-aula."

"And will they do your bidding?" Eleio asked again. The older man nodded.

"Do as I say," Eleio spoke, "and perhaps Kanikani-aula can come and live among her people once again."

Eleio instructed them to build a great arbor and decorate it with the sweetest-smelling flowers on the island. Inside the arbor they were to erect an altar, then prepare a feast. They were to cook the hog and lay it on the altar together with red and white fish, red, white and black chickens and

different kinds of banana. They were to lock away in their houses all their pigs, chickens and dogs, and to observe a strict silence as they went about their work and prayer.

While these preparations were taking place, Eleio ran quickly across to Hana and pulled from the ground bushes of kava, a plant of great medicinal strength. When Eleio returned to the village, the preparations were completed. Eleio caught sight of the spirit of Kanikani-aula. She lingered close behind him, though no one else could see her.

Eleio fixed a preparation from the kava plant. Then he entered the flower-strewn arbor where he offered his prayers and began to call upon the gods. As he chanted the final words, Eleio turned and took the spirit of Kanikani-aula by the hand. He led her out of the arbor and back to the poua. There he lifted her gently, her spirit lying across his arms like a long white cloud, and carefully began to press the spirit back into her body as he chanted.

Kanikani-aula's family stood patiently beneath the poua. They could hear Eleio's chanting. His voice was carried by the wind and mingled with the churning hiss of the waves as they tumbled against the cliffs. Suddenly the chanting stopped and when the

people looked up, standing above them was Kanikani-aula, radiant and smiling. Kanikani-aula's family wept for joy and she was taken to the priest for a ceremony of purification.

That evening there was a huge feast. The food spilt from the groaning platters and there was joyful singing and dancing. After the feast, the feather cloak, the rolls of tapa cloth and the beautiful mats were brought and laid before Eleio.

"Eleio, take these gifts for we owe you much," Kanikani-aula's father addressed him. "Come and live with our family, take Kanikani-aula as your wife and be a son to us."

Eleio looked toward the beautiful Kanikani-aula — he had never seen a woman as striking as her. Then he looked down at the fine gifts before him and he spoke. "Kanikani-aula is worthy of a husband of much higher rank than I. If you would entrust her to my care, I will take her to my chief, Kakaalaneo. For her beauty and her charms make her worthy to be his wife and our queen."

Eleio then turned to Kanikani-aula. "Kanikani-aula, finish this feather cloak for I have never seen one like it before, and neither has my chief. It is a valuable gift."

At once, all those who knew the art began to work upon the cloak using the beautiful red feathers of the parrot. As soon as it was finished, Eleio and Kanikani-aula set off to Chief Kakaalaneo's village, carrying between them the gifts of the tapa cloth, the mats and the feather cloak. As they neared the village, Eleio turned to Kanikani-aula and said, "Wait here hidden in these bushes. If by sundown I have not returned, all is not well and you must return to your own people. Follow the path that we have just taken."

Then, taking the gifts, Eleio continued toward the chieftain's whare. Ahead of him he saw a group of people heating an imu, an oven set in the ground. When they saw Eleio, they came and took hold of him roughly, saying, "Eleio, Chief Kakaalaneo is very angry at you for not returning with the kava root. He has ordered that we should roast you alive!"

Eleio answered, "If I am to die, then let me die at the feet of my chief."

The people, being fond of Eleio, took him before the chief.

"Why is this man not dead? What is he doing standing here before me?" the chief roared when he saw Eleio.

"It was my wish," explained Eleio, "that if I should die I should die at your feet. But please, before you kill me, see the wondrous gifts that I have brought you." And Eleio placed before the chief the tapa cloth, the mats and the feather cloak.

The striking red-feather cloak immediately caught the chief's attention. He was quite astonished by the garment. Of course Eleio was pardoned and welcomed when he produced the remaining kava plants that he had fetched during his time with Kanikani-aula's family. When the chief heard Eleio's story, he grew curious. He ordered Eleio to bring before him the woman who had made the cloak so that he might see her for himself and express his gratitude for the wonderful garment.

Quickly Eleio returned and fetched Kanikani-aula from her hiding place. When Chief Kakaalaneo saw Kanikani-aula, he was immediately charmed by her and understood why Eleio had wanted to restore her to life. He

could also see that Eleio and Kanikani-aula had fallen in love with each other, and he insisted that the young couple marry.

So Kanikani-aula was brought back from the dead by Eleio and became celebrated as the creator of the first feather cloak. The descendants of Eleio and Kanikani-aula live even now on the islands of Hawaii and it is said that the feather cloak, known as Ahu O Kakaalaneo, is preserved to this day.

The Story of Flax

Flax was probably the first vegetable fiber to be used in the production of fabric. Remnants of flax cloth dating from 5000 BC have been found in Egyptian tombs, and linen is mentioned on several occasions in the Old Testament. Jewish, Egyptian, and Greek priests all wore linen to symbolize purity.

Flax was brought from western Asia to Europe by the Romans, and linen became the chief European textile of the Middle Ages. Today flax is cultivated all over the world.

The flax plant grows 3 to 4 feet in height and has blue or white flowers. During harvesting the plant is pulled from the ground, rather than cut, to obtain the longest possible fibers. Once harvested, the sheaves of flax are left to dry before retting — soaking the plant in water — takes place. This process helps remove the woody matter of the plant from the workable fibers. Historically, retting was done in waterways. However, in Britain during the reign of Henry VIII, retting was forbidden in rivers as it polluted the water too badly.

After retting, the sheaves are arranged in shocks to drain and then spread out to dry. Next, the dressing of the flax takes place. The fibers are broken, scrutched, and hackled. Scrutching is the separation of stalks from the fibers, and

50

hackling is the massing of the fibers through a series of increasingly fine metal cones. The long threads are then stored in bundles, ready for spinning. Bleaching, weaving, and finishing processes vary depending on whether the final product is to be a coarse fabric, such as sailcloth, canvas, or sacking, or a delicate one, such as cambric or lawn — like the cloth created by the three old "aunts" in the story.

Many superstitions surround flax. To dream of the plant indicates a happy and prosperous marriage. To dream of spinning flax, however, suggests bad fortune. When it blooms, flax can be cut for use as a protection against witchcraft. It can also be woven with chants and incantations to protect the wearer of the final garment.

In Scandinavia, where this story originates, flax was under the protection of the goddess Hulda. She was said to be the one who first taught mortals to grow, spin, and weave flax. In summer, when the flax was blooming, it was said that she would pass down through the valleys blessing the crops. Hulda is also the queen of the fairy women who watch over the flax plants. On the twelve days before Christmas, when spinning was not permitted, Hulda was said to visit the houses to examine the distaffs of the spinning wheels. She was also believed to reward industrious spinners and punish lazy ones. It is likely that the three old women in this story (the three "fayes") are fairy guardians of the flax.

The Three Fayes

Swedish

In a small cottage there lived a widow woman and her daughter, May. Although May was smart and beautiful, she did not enjoy spinning as her mother did. The older woman would spend all her time at the spinning wheel, spinning flax into skeins. But the young daughter preferred to work outside, tending their garden and looking after the animals.

Her mother would scold her. "What hope have you of ever finding a husband!" she would say. "Skeins of flax are the only dowry we can offer."

As the years passed, she grew more and more impatient with her daughter. No matter how hard May worked outside, all her mother wanted was to have her indoors. She would shout at the girl and threaten her, but nothing would bring May to the wheel to spin. One morning the mother grew so cross with her daughter that she picked up a switch and started to chase her around the house. Poor May began to weep loudly and begged her mother to put down the switch.

Now it just so happened that that very morning the queen was passing through the town in her carriage. When she heard the sound of crying, she stopped her carriage and knocked on the cottage door.

The mother trembled when she saw the queen. Ashamed of her anger, she lied: "Your Majesty, my daughter is such a keen spinner I cannot pull her from the spinning wheel and must threaten her with a beating. Alas, we are very poor and I have not enough flax for her to spin. That is why you heard her weeping."

The queen looked at the young woman, and although the girl's eyes were swollen from crying, she could see that May was very pretty.

"I like nothing better than to listen to the hum of the spinning wheel. Let me take your daughter to the palace. There is no shortage of flax there and she can spin to her heart's content."

As they set off in the queen's carriage, May waved sadly at her mother standing by the cottage door. The mother watched her daughter go, tears rolling down her face. Although she had been angry with May, she was heartbroken to lose her. But who can refuse a queen?

On arriving at the palace, May was led into a huge room. The sight that greeted her made her gasp with dismay, for the whole room was filled with flax, from floor to ceiling, and in one corner stood a spinning wheel.

"If you spin all this flax for me," said the queen, "you shall be handsomely rewarded, for I shall give you my eldest son as your husband. You may be poor, but hard work is the best dowry a woman can offer."

With that, the queen swept out of the room. May knew that she would never be able to spin even a tiny part of all that flax. She looked at the hateful spinning wheel, dropped down onto the spinning stool and began to sob in utter despair.

Then, all of a sudden, there came a strange sound: step, thump, step, thump. May looked up and saw, standing right in front of her, a small, very odd-looking woman. Her body was crooked and misshapen, but the most striking thing about her was her huge foot. Why, it was nearly as long as the old woman was tall! May tried not to stare; instead she wiped her eyes and greeted her kindly: "Blessings be upon you, Mother."

"And blessings be upon you, child," replied the old woman. "Tell me, why do you sit here weeping?"

"I weep, Mother, because I fear my good fortune has deserted me. I have been asked by the queen herself to spin all this flax, and yet I can spin about as well as the devil can pray."

"Aah, fear not, my child," replied the old woman, "for I will spin all the flax for you this very night. All I ask in return is that you should call me Aunt and invite me to sit at your table on your wedding day, without feeling any shame."

May promised faithfully that she would do what the old woman asked and in that instant she fell into a deep sleep. When she awoke the next morning, her eyes widened with astonishment. All around her, stacked in neat piles, were hundreds of newly spun skeins, yet there was no sign of the strange old woman. At that moment there came a loud knock at the door, and the queen entered. She was scarcely less surprised than May to see all the skeins of flax, but she congratulated the girl.

"Clearly you are a skillful spinner, but how well can you throw the shuttle?"

The queen called for her attendants and the spinning wheel was taken from the room and a loom set in its place. "Weave these skeins into cloth," she said, "and I shall set a wedding day for you and my son."

Again the queen departed. May walked across the room and picked up the shuttle. She did not even know how to thread the warp threads onto the loom. Burying her face in her hands, she began to weep bitterly. If she could hardly spin, then weaving was a complete mystery to her.

Then, all of a sudden, she felt the touch of a hand on her shoulder.

Startled, she looked up and saw standing beside her another old woman as peculiar looking as the first. Although she did not have a huge paddle foot, this old woman was nearly doubled over, so hunched was her back.

"Blessings be upon you, Mother," said May. "But you did give me a fright!"

"And blessings be upon you, child. I hope I did not alarm you too much. Tell me, why do you sit here weeping?"

"I weep, Mother, because my fortune twists first one way then another. The queen has promised me her eldest son in marriage, but first I must weave these skeins of flax into cloth, and I do not know where to begin."

"Rest yourself," said the old woman, "for I shall weave the cloth for you this very night. All I ask in return is that you should call me Aunt and invite me to sit at your table on your wedding day, without feeling any shame."

May agreed at once, and once again she fell fast asleep. When she awoke the next morning, she saw rolled up in several bales alongside her the most beautifully woven flax cloth. Just as May was reaching out a hand to touch the wondrous fabric, there came a knock on the door, and the queen entered.

Although she dressed daily in the finest and most expensive clothes, the queen had never seen such exquisite fabric. She took a bale of cloth to the window and held it up to the light.

"Fine work, May," she said. "This cloth is fine enough to make the shirt for a prince to wear on his wedding day."

The queen's attendants busied themselves removing the loom, and in its place they set a table, laying on it needles, pins, scissors, and thread.

"One final task," the queen continued. "Sew me a shirt from this cloth and I will make you a princess."

As soon as the queen had gone, May took a bale of cloth and spread it across the table. She had seen plenty of shirts in her life, but had never before attempted to make one. As she stood there, staring helplessly at the cloth, a third old woman suddenly appeared in the room. Her hands were clasped in front of her and May could not help but notice her huge thumb.

"Blessings be upon you, Mother," said May.

"And blessings be upon you, my child. Tell me: why do you look so miserable?"

"Aah, Mother, I have an impossible task before me. The queen has asked me to make a shirt for the prince to wear on his wedding day, and if I succeed, I shall be his bride. But I am so ignorant: if the queen had asked me to pluck her a star from the heavens, I would have stood a better chance of success."

"Fret not, child," replied the old woman, "for I shall shape you a shirt from this cloth. All I ask in return is that you should call me Aunt and invite me to sit at your table on your wedding day, without feeling any shame."

Well, of course May agreed, and sleep spread over her at once. She dreamed of the prince and of a grand wedding. When she awoke, she saw

lying on the table a shirt of such exquisite quality that kings would have fought each other to possess it. The stitching was so fine that the seams were invisible, and the buttons shone like pearls. May gave a gasp of delight. Then there came a knock at the door and the queen herself was standing beside her, marveling at the workmanship.

"If you turn out to be as fine a wife as you are a seamstress, my son will be a lucky man," she said to May. Then, taking her by the hand, the queen led her from the room.

When the prince and May set eyes on each another, they fell in love. Whenever May looked at the prince, her heart beat faster, and whenever the prince caught sight of May, a warm feeling swept through him. Soon the palace was a flurry of activity as preparations were made for the wedding.

"All I ask is that my mother and my three old aunts be invited," was May's only request amid the hustle and bustle of the preparations.

On the day of the wedding, great crowds lined the streets to wish the bridal couple well and to catch a glimpse of the guests. Carriage after carriage rolled past, shining with silver and gold, and from them stepped the most gorgeously dressed men and women, adorned in silk, velvet, and satin.

Last of all came a very strange carriage. It was made from an enormous gourd and was drawn by several pairs of large white mice. From this carriage stepped the three old women: the first with her huge paddle foot, the second with her hunched back, and the third with her enormous thumb. May stepped forward and greeted them warmly, while the king, queen, and prince looked on in amazement.

After the wedding service, May invited her three aunts to sit with the royal family at the head table. Their plates were piled high and the old women ate their fill. The prince could not take his eyes off the three strange guests. Unable to contain his curiosity any longer, he turned to the first aunt.

"Excuse me, Mother, but how did your foot come to be so large?"

"From spinning, my son," the first old woman replied. "The pedal of the wheel has caused my foot to spread and thicken to its present size."

I should hate my wife to have such a foot, the prince thought to himself. Then he turned to the second aunt. "And you, Mother, how did your back come to be so bent and crooked?"

"From weaving, my son," replied the second old woman. "From stooping over the loom and throwing the shuttle."

My wife shall never lay her hands on a loom again, the prince thought to himself. And finally he addressed the third aunt. "Your thumb, Mother. How did it come to grow so large?"

"From sewing, my son," replied the third old woman. "From licking and twisting the thread."

Thanking the three old aunts, the prince turned his attention back to May. Then, as all the guests raised their brimming goblets to give congratulations and blessings to the married couple, he announced that never again would his wife spin, weave, or sew another stitch for as long as she lived.

May never did spin, weave, or sew another stitch, and she and the prince lived happily together for many years, although in all that time she never saw the three old aunts again.

58

Patchwork & Quilting

Patchwork was born out of necessity, but it developed into an art form in its own right. Before the invention of industrial looms, textiles were expensive and highly prized. So in most households, clothes and furnishings were carefully repaired with protective patches.

Pieced work, or patchwork, may well predate weaving. Inuit women patch the furs that they wear with smaller pieces, and Stone Age people probably did the same. There is evidence, too, that patchwork was used by ancient civilizations such as the Egyptians and Assyrians. In the Old Testament, Joseph's famous coat of many colors could well have been made of patchwork. Historic Palestine, Holy Land of the Jews, Christians and Muslims, has a long history of patchworking. In the Middle Ages, Crusaders brought the technique back to Europe with them, where it became a popular way of making dresses, wall and bed hangings and church decorations.

Quilting — the stitching together of two layers of fabric with a soft, thick material such as cotton or wool between — has also been used since ancient times in many parts of the world, especially China, India and the Middle East. It was

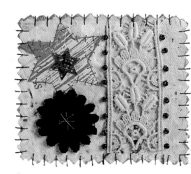

60

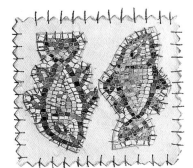

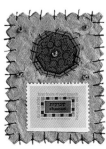

used for military doublets underneath armor, and could even be a substitute for armor. In fourteenth-century Europe, the quilting of bedcovers became quite an art form, but it reached its fullest expression in North America during the nineteenth century. Here, the production of a quilt was done in a group, or quilting bee, often as a wedding gift for a young couple. Patchwork quilting is a good example of the mutual help that was so critical to the survival of the early pioneers.

Different regions developed their own distinctive designs and patterns, often reflecting the quilters' ethnic origins. The log cabin was a very popular design: strips of fabric were joined to form a square, which was said to represent the hearth and the home. However, it was not just the patterns that told the story. The actual choice of cloth and process of creating a quilt were a record of the life of the quilter, whose story was recorded in cloth and handed down through the generations:

"It took me more than twenty years, nearly twenty-five I reckon, in the evening after supper, when the children were all put to bed. My whole life is in that quilt. It scares me sometimes when I look at it. All my joys and all my sorrows are stitched into those little pieces...I tremble sometimes when I remember what that quilt knows about me."
— Marguerite Ickis, *America's Quilts and Coverlets.*

61

The Patchwork Coat

Jewish

There was once a man by the name of Khaim Yankl. He was so poor that when the wind blew it whistled through the walls of his house and chilled him to the bone. He was so poor that when the heavens poured rain down onto this earth, the water would drip and drop through the holes in his ceiling and form large puddles on the floor. He was so poor that there was hardly a scrap or a speck of food to feed his wife and his six children. They were all very hungry and cold.

Finally Khaim Yankl thought to himself: "This is no way for a man to live. I shall set off this minute into the world to beg for alms."

So, bidding his family farewell, Khaim Yankl strode away with his fiddle under one arm. He walked for days, through forests, towns and villages.

In some towns and villages, Khaim Yankl would sit with his hands stretched out to passers-by and occasionally one would throw him a coin that he would tuck away deep in his pocket. Sometimes he would take his fiddle and play in the marketplace, and quickly a crowd would form about him as he teased from those strings sad tunes of longing or bright happy jigs. These tunes would always bring a generous shower of coins.

In the countryside, Khaim Yankl would take odd jobs — fixing, cleaning or digging. He would turn his hand to whatever was available, and it wasn't long before his pockets were jangling with coins.

But with his new wealth came worry. Soon the coins grew too heavy. Anxious for their safety, Khaim Yankl took them out and exchanged them for paper money. Then he worried again, for he could not think of a safe place to put the bills. He worried about robbers stealing them, about losing the money, about the wind snatching the bills away. Finally he had an idea. He took a needle, some thread and a patch of cloth. Carefully he stitched the patch to his old coat, leaving one end open. In through the open end he slipped several of the bills, then he sealed the opening with a few extra stitches. After that he took another patch and did the same thing again. Who would ever guess the secret contained in Khaim Yankl's old coat?

As the days and weeks passed, Khaim Yankl's coat became covered in patchwork squares of all kinds: woolen, linen and moleskin, red, yellow and blue, floral, spotted and striped. Each patch concealed a healthy wad of bills. He sewed patches on the sleeves, on the collar, the pockets and on the lining inside. Khaim Yankl now had a padded patchwork coat.

So the years passed. Khaim Yankl did not notice how quickly time slipped by. Soon his family became convinced that he was dead. His wife took in laundry and scrubbed floors to feed the family, and, as the children came of age, they did what they could to earn a few coins.

Twenty years passed. By this time, Khaim Yankl was a wealthy man. Suddenly he realized it was high time he returned home. He bought himself a beautiful new coat with a fur-trimmed collar, a pair of smart trousers, a crisp linen shirt and strong leather boots. Then, bundling his old coat up under his arm, he set off.

When he arrived at his village, nobody recognized him. He walked down the street to his house. He knocked loudly on the front door, the paint now peeling off it. It was answered by a young woman. Khaim Yankl recognized

63

her as one of his own dear daughters, now stretched tall by the passing of years. But she did not recognize him in his smart new clothes.

"May I speak to your father?" he asked.

"I have no father," the young woman explained. "He set off to seek his fortune twenty years ago and has never returned. I think he may be dead."

"No!" cried Khaim Yankl in great happiness. "I am your father!" And he embraced her warmly.

Well, the news spread quickly. His children all came to greet him, and up and down the street the neighbors called, "Khaim Yankl is back — he is a millionaire!"

Khaim Yankl's wife was away from home, hard at work scrubbing floors. When she heard the news, she refused to believe it. How could it be her husband after all these years? By the time she reached home, Khaim Yankl had gone to visit the synagogue to offer his prayers. He had left the patchwork coat hanging on a peg in the corner of the kitchen and his prayer shawl, forgotten, on the kitchen table.

When Khaim Yankl's wife walked into the kitchen, the shawl was the first thing she saw. Astonished, she picked it up and held it out in front of her.

She studied the familiar fabric, a little worn after the passing of the years. She studied the needlework and the corner she had patched herself and instantly recognized it as being her husband's own shawl. Quickly she began to go about the kitchen preparing the midday meal, her heart in her mouth.

As she went about her work, she was startled by a loud knocking at the door. Outside stood a poor man asking for alms. Well, of course Khaim Yankl's wife had nothing to give the man but, thinking of her own husband, she was reluctant to send him away empty-handed. Looking about the kitchen, her eyes fell upon the patchwork coat hanging on the peg in the corner. It was the oldest, filthiest piece of clothing she had ever seen.

"Here," she said, passing the patchwork coat to the beggar. "It is very old and probably not much use, but please take it with my blessing."

The poor man thanked Khaim Yankl's wife and, wrapping the coat about himself, walked away.

Not long after, Khaim Yankl returned from the synagogue and what tears of joy were shed between himself and his wife. They embraced, they talked

65

and they ate. And the whole family sat and listened to their father's story. They could hardly believe that it was truly him that sat there with them at the table.

When the meal was finished and the plates cleared away, Khaim Yankl took from his pocket a knife and began to sharpen it on a stone. Suddenly the family's joy turned to terror. What if this man was not Khaim Yankl? Perhaps he was a robber who had come to murder them?

Khaim Yankl stood up and walked to the corner of the kitchen. His wife and children huddled together at the opposite end of the room, while one son stood near the front door, ready to run and fetch help should it be needed. Seeing the empty peg where he had left his old coat hanging, Khaim Yankl searched in vain all around the kitchen.

"Wife," he called, "have you seen a patchwork coat?"

The wife's heart was pounding but she replied, "You mean that dirty old patchwork coat? Why, I gave it away to a beggarman who came to our door."

When Khaim Yankl heard these words, he fainted dead away. Quickly his family forgot their fear and crowded about him, splashing his face with water and slapping his cheeks. When finally he came to, he said, "Aah, my whole fortune, all the money I collected over these past twenty years — all inside that coat!"

When Khaim Yankl's wife heard this, she too fainted dead away. Khaim Yankl stood up at once, donned his new coat, took his fiddle and walked out of the house. He strode down to the town square and began to play on his fiddle and this is the song he sang:

> "*I am a fool, an old fool,*
> *Gray and unwise;*
> *I am a fool, I am a fool,*
> *And I tell you no lies.*"

Soon people gathered around him and they whispered among themselves: "Khaim Yankl — what is wrong with him, has he gone quite mad?"

But Khaim Yankl kept singing:

"I am a fool, an old fool,
Foolish yet jolly;
With my tongue and my fiddle
I'll sing you my folly."

People began to call out, "Khaim Yankl, have you gone mad playing your fiddle in the middle of the day?"

Soon the whole town had gathered around to watch the spectacle. Storekeepers, mothers with children, men on their way home to their supper — they all stopped and watched. Among them was the beggarman wearing Khaim Yankl's patchwork coat.

Khaim Yankl caught sight of the coat — a flurry of bright colors amid the crowd. He stopped playing his fiddle and shouted, "Good people, let me show you how great a fool I am. You, kind sir," he pointed to the beggarman, "let us exchange coats. I will give you my new coat for your old one."

A roar of laughter rippled through the crowd. What kind of man would exchange his beautiful expensive new coat with a fur-trimmed collar for an old patchwork one? The poor man was delighted, of course. He pushed to the front of the crowd. Peeling off the old coat, he handed it to Khaim Yankl and there on the spot the men traded coats.

It was difficult to tell which man looked more pleased, Khaim Yankl or the beggar. But the poor man, fearing that Khaim Yankl might change his mind, quickly ran away. Khaim Yankl again picked up his fiddle and began walking home, singing aloud:

> *"He's a fool, he's a fool*
> *For he knows not my secret:*
> *There's a fortune patched here;*
> *In thanking him I'll keep it!"*

By the time Khaim Yankl reached home, the crowd had died away. He went into the kitchen and, taking up the knife once again, he unpicked the seams holding the patches. Patch by patch, he peeled the pieces of cloth from the coat. His family watched in amazement as a great pile of bills steadily mounted on the table.

From that day on, Khaim Yankl and his family lived like wealthy people, never wishing, never wanting, but always grateful for what they had. As for the patchwork coat, it was repaired and hung on the peg in the corner of the kitchen. Khaim Yankl would never hear of throwing it away.

Batik-Making in Java

Indonesia is famous for its batik. This characteristic national cloth is primarily produced on the island of Java. Scholars cannot agree when batik production first began in Java. However, the process is hundreds of years old: remnants of batik cloth dating from 1500 BC have been found in both Egypt and the Middle East.

70

The intricate patterns, or tulis, of batik are painted on using a pen-like wax holder called a canting, or by applying wax to the cloth with a copper stamp or "cap." The recipes for this wax mixture are fiercely guarded secrets. When the melted wax has been applied to the cloth — traditionally cotton or silk — and has had time to dry, the cloth is ready to be dyed. The wax makes the cloth resistant to the dye, so only the unwaxed areas absorb the color. The process can be repeated several times with different dyes, wax designs being added to or scraped from the cloth between dyeing sessions to achieve a complex and striking range of patterns and colors.

Many superstitions are associated with dyeing the cloth in order to guarantee a rich color. Chicken meat, rainwater, or ashes from the kitchen fire may be added to ward off evil spirits. Domestic arguments should be avoided.

Traditionally, the most common dye is indigo, made from the leaves of the indigo plant. Other natural dyes include brown from the soga tree, yellow from the jirak tree and a deep red called mengkudu from the leaves of the *Morinda citrifolia*.

Over three thousand patterns can be found in batik design. Popular ones include diamonds and circlets and many different animal and plant forms. Some designs are regional, while others denote status, are reserved for royalty or are believed to have magical functions.

71

When Damura, the heroine of this story, steps from the mouth of the crocodile, radiantly dressed for the feast, she is wearing prada cloth. This is batik cloth that has been decorated with gold dust, applied using a mixture of egg white. Prada is reserved for festive occasions and for ceremonial use. The kabaya that Damura wears is a type of lace shirt worn by Indonesian women on special occasions.

Traditional items of clothing that are dyed using the batik method include the kain sarong, a tubular cloth worn on a daily basis by both men and woman; the selendang, a long, narrow cloth used as a shawl or as a carryall for children or shopping by women only; the iket kepala, a square head-cloth worn by men in a turban-like fashion; and the kemben, a woman's breast cloth. The dodot sarong is a ceremonial sarong up to six times the length of a kain sarong. It is often worn by the bride and groom on their wedding day.

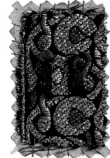

The Crocodile's Blessing

Indonesian

Once there was a beautiful young girl called Damura, who lived with her father, stepmother, and stepsister in a village by the edge of a great river. Everyone loved Damura. She always had a piece of fruit to share with the children who played on the streets, rice for the poor and a comforting word for the elderly. As she went about her work, she would sing happily and the birds and butterflies would hover above her in a halo of rainbow colors.

Damura's father was a fisherman whose work often took him far away. Then Damura's stepmother gave Damura the hardest work to do. But Damura never complained. As the years passed, Damura grew into a handsome young woman. Soon suitors would be lining up outside the home to ask the old fisherman for his daughter's hand in marriage.

One day, Damura's stepmother called her to her. "Damura, the head of the village is coming for a meal tomorrow. You are to take all the furnishings and our clothes down to the river and scrub them well," she ordered.

Damura had done all the household washing only two days ago, but she also knew it was pointless to argue with her stepmother. So she gathered together all she needed and walked down to the river.

But as she began washing her stepmother's finest sarong, the fast-flowing current snatched the cloth from her hands and swept it downstream. Damura gave a cry of despair. The river was deep and the current was strong, and the sarong quickly swept round a bend in the river. What was Damura to do? Heaving the basket of washing up higher onto the bank, she set off after the sarong, hoping that the river might sweep it up onto the bank further downstream. She walked for hours along the riverbank until the sun sank low in the west. Then she sat down and began to weep.

"Damura, why are you weeping here by the river?" came a voice. "Is the sea not salty enough?"

Damura looked up. As she gazed out across the water, she noticed two large saucer-like eyes peering at her. They were the eyes of a crocodile. Damura was frightened of crocodiles but she answered politely, "How kind you are, Crocodile, to spare a thought for me. Had I known my tears were disturbing you, I would have caught them all. But I fear they may be too many even for the sea, for the river has taken my stepmother's finest sarong, and I dare not return home without it."

"Damura," the crocodile replied, "do not despair. I will help you, but first you must help me. Climb upon my back."

Damura hesitated; the crocodile was large, with big gleaming teeth. Still, better to be eaten by a crocodile than to return home without the sarong. She waded out into the water and climbed onto the crocodile's back.

"Hold on tightly, Damura," the crocodile called as it flicked its long leathery tail and dived under the water. The silty brown water of the river filled Damura's eyes and nose but she held on tightly. Soon the crocodile resurfaced by a cave of branches. It slapped its tail loudly and from the cave appeared a baby crocodile.

"Damura, if you sit here and mind my child, I will find the lost sarong for you," the crocodile said. Damura nodded and for a second time the crocodile disappeared beneath the surface of the river.

73

Damura sat down by the baby crocodile, who curled up alongside. She began to sing the baby songs of the river and sea. She sang about the crocodiles who lived in the river, about their swiftness, strength, and cunning, about the warm sun that caressed their bodies. She sang of the sweetness of the baby crocodile, and finally the baby crocodile fell asleep.

"Ah, Damura, you have taken good care of my baby," came the voice of the mother crocodile, "and I have found your sarong." Sure enough, there in the crocodile's mouth was the sarong. Damura thanked the crocodile.

"From your mouth comes only sweetness," replied the crocodile, "and I will make it sweeter still. Drink from the river, Damura, and speak to no one until you reach your home."

Damura did as she was told. Then the crocodile carried her back to the bank where her basket stood, the washing all clean, dry, and neatly folded.

Damura hurried home. Just as she was about to explain why she was so late, gold coins showered from her mouth to the floor. The stepmother and her father listened in amazement as Damura told them of her adventure. The stepmother resolved to send her own daughter to the river.

The next morning, the stepdaughter took the basket of washing down to the river. She was a lazy girl and for a time she sat on the banks of the river

playing with her hair. After a while, she picked out her mother's finest sarong and hurled it out into the middle of the river. Then she began to walk downstream. The branches caught on her blouse and snagged in her hair and she cursed the river and the trouble it was causing her. Scratched and disheveled, she sat down and began to cry.

"Why do you cry?" came a deep, watery voice. "Is the sea not salty enough?"

"Why shouldn't I cry!" the stepdaughter snapped back at the crocodile. "Look at my clothes — all ripped and ragged; and my skin — all specked and lumpy with mosquito bites. And look at me — forced to walk along this river to find my mother's sarong!"

"Do not speak so unkindly of your fate. I will help you if you will help me," replied the crocodile. "Just climb onto my back."

The girl clambered ungraciously onto the crocodile's back. "Ooooh, how clammy and cold your skin is!" she cried.

The crocodile flicked its long tail and dived under the water. The stepdaughter opened her mouth to scream but the silty brown water rushed in and choked her. Spluttering and cursing, the girl surfaced on the crocodile's back outside the cave of branches. Again the crocodile struck its tail on the riverbank and the baby crocodile appeared.

"If you will sit here and look after my baby, I will go and look for your sarong," said the crocodile. Then it disappeared back into the river.

"Horrible lizard," hissed the girl as she pushed the baby crocodile away with one foot. "You stay away from me, you nasty, slimy creature."

The stepdaughter perched on a rock where the baby could not reach her and began to sing. But her songs were bitter and full of complaint. The baby crocodile began to wail and call for its mother, who immediately surfaced from the river, the sarong wet and limp in her mouth.

"From your mouth comes only filth," growled the crocodile, "and you have made my baby cry. Drink from this river to wash those foul words away, and mind you speak to no one until you reach home."

The stepdaughter took a small sip from the river then snatched the sarong from the crocodile. Scrambling back along the bank to the basket of washing, she found that it had been tipped over and the clothes were soiled and wet. Angrily she stomped home. As she stumbled in through the door of the house, she was greeted by her parents and the head of the village. The girl was scratched, ragged, muddy, and wet, and when she spoke not gold but rocks fell from her mouth. Damura hurried from the kitchen to take the basket of soiled laundry from her sister and to comfort her.

The village head looked at the stepdaughter with surprise and at Damura with admiration. Then, turning politely to the parents, he exclaimed, "What beautiful daughters you have! I would be most pleased if you would all attend a feast that I am holding in my son's honor."

For the next week there was nothing but talk of the feast.

"Of course, Damura, it will be impossible for you to go, for you have nothing to wear," said the stepmother unkindly to the girl.

With a heavy heart, Damura continued to help her stepmother and sister prepare for the feast. They wore the finest, brightly colored sarongs and lace kebayas. Bracelets and rings encircled their wrists and fingers, and Damura brushed their long dark hair until it shone.

"Where is Damura?" asked the father as they were about to leave.

"Ah, poor Damura," lied the stepmother, "she does not feel well and so will not be joining us this evening."

Once they had left, Damura walked down to the river and sat on the bank. She stared up at the silvery moon and a tear rolled down her face.

"Ah, Damura, why do you weep?" came a familiar voice. "Is the sea not salty enough?"

"Oh, Crocodile, it is you. How kind you have been to me. But there is little kindness in my world," sighed Damura. "My family have gone to the feast, but I am here alone for I have nothing to wear."

"Do not weep, Damura, for I will help you," smiled the crocodile. "Come a little closer and climb into my mouth."

Damura walked toward the crocodile although her legs trembled with fear. She lifted the skirts of her sarong and stepped inside the huge yawning mouth of the crocodile. Gleaming in the darkness, she saw a finely woven prada cloth, the batik glittering with painted gold leaf, the finest lace kabaya, a jacket of golden silk, and dainty golden sandals.

"Dress yourself quickly," came the crocodile's low, rumbling voice.

When Damura stepped from the mouth of the crocodile, she was as radiant as the moon itself. Her hair gleamed thick and dark like the night river and her eyes twinkled like the stars above.

The crocodile thumped its tail twice on the riverbank and Damura found herself standing outside the house of the village head. From inside came the sound of music and laughter. The aroma of rich food and fresh tropical fruit filled the night air. Sitting alone outside was the son of the village head. He was handsomely dressed but he seemed bored and unhappy. When he caught sight of Damura, he smiled.

"I see that you, too, are hiding from all the noise and people," he said to her. "It is like a room full of monkeys."

Damura laughed and the young man invited her to sit with him. All evening the two of them talked, but at dawn, Damura stood up to leave.

"I have never known an evening to be so short or so interesting," exclaimed the son of the village head, taking Damura by the hand. "Please tell me your name and where you come from so that I may see you again."

Fearing her stepmother's anger, Damura shook her head and ran from the house, but in her hurry one of her golden sandals fell from her foot and lay in the dust. The son of the village head ran after Damura and stumbled upon the fallen sandal. He examined the beautifully crafted shoe with sorrow. Would he ever see its owner again? Returning to his father's house, he declared that he would marry the woman who possessed the other sandal.

The village head sent his servants out into the village. At each house, they were greeted by eager women who tried desperately to convince the servants that the sandal was indeed theirs. But the sandal would fit no one and the other shoe was nowhere to be found.

Finally the servants knocked upon the door of the small house on the edge of the river. Damura answered but was quickly pushed aside by her stepmother and sister. Both tried the sandal but their feet were too coarse and large to fit it.

"What about the young woman in the corner?" motioned the servant.

"What? Damura?" they snorted. "She didn't even go to the feast."

But the servant stretched out the sandal toward Damura, who took it and slipped it on her foot. Then she reached into the folds of her sarong and took out the other sandal. The stepmother and daughter looked on with a mixture of surprise and horror.

"I shall take you now to the house of the village head," smiled the servant.

Damura and the son of the village head were married at once, and they lived together in great contentment. As long as the river was their happiness, and as deep as the sea was their love.

Sources

CLEVER ANAEET

This story is a hybrid tale, bringing together the best of Armenian and Persian variations of a similar story. The original Armenian version of the story can be found in James Riordan's *The World of Folktales* (Hamlyn, London, 1981) and the Persian version in Anita Stern's *World Folktales: An Anthology of Multicultural Folk Literature* (National Text Book Company, Illinois, 1994).

THE CLOTH OF THE SERPENT PEMBE MIRUI

I came across this unique Swahili tale in Roger D. Abraham's *African Folktales: Traditional Stories of the Black Worlds* (Pantheon Books, New York, 1983). Similarities with the more familiar "Puss-in-Boots" story can be seen in the relationship between Amadi and the resourceful cat.

THE SILK BROCADE

This well-known Chinese story is a popular choice for fairytale collections. Though I first heard this story told orally, versions of the tale can be found in Joanna Cole's *Best Loved Folktales of the World* (Anchor Books, London and New York, 1982) and He Liyu's *The Spring of Butterflies and other Chinese Folktales* (Collins, London, 1985).

THE FEATHER CLOAK

Having been born in the South Pacific, I was determined to include a tale from this beautiful part of the world. I first came across this story in Johannes C. Andersen's *Myths and Legends of the Polynesians* (George G. Harrap and Company, Edinburgh, 1928).

THE THREE FAYES

This story is a Nordic variation on Grimms' "The Three Spinners" (*The Complete Grimms' Fairytales, Routledge*, London, 1983; see also George Stephens and H. Cavallius, *Old Norse Fairytales*, W. Swan Sonnerschein & Co., London, 1880s). It also has similarities with the well-known "Rumpelstiltskin" tale, with the three benevolent fairy helpers in place of the bad-tempered little man.

THE PATCHWORK COAT

This delightful story can be found in Leonard Wolf's excellent collection, *Yiddish Folktales*, edited by Beatrice Silverman Weinreich (Yivo Institute/Pantheon Books, New York, 1988).

THE CROCODILE'S BLESSING

This is one of many versions of the Cinderella tale that are told throughout the world. The "seed" of this tale came from Jan Knappert's *Pacific Mythology* (Aquarian Press, London and New York, 1992).

80

Bibliography

Baines, Patricia, *Spinning Wheels, Spinners and Spinning*, Batsford, London, 1977.

Bisighani, J. D., *Hawaii Handbook*, Moon Publishers, Chico, 1989.

Bushnaq, Inea (tr. and ed.), *Arab Folktales*, Pantheon Books, New York, 1986.

Colby, Averil, *Patchwork*, Anchor Press, London, 1958.

Edwards, Philip (ed.), *The Journals of Captain Cook*, Penguin, London, 1999.

Folkard, Richard, *Plant Lore Legends and Lyrics*, Sampson Low, Marston & Co., St. Dunstans House, London, 1884.

Fraser-Lu, Sylvia, *Indonesian Batik: Processes, Pattern and Places*, Oxford University Press, Oxford, 1986.

Gilchrist, Cherry, *Stories from the Silk Road*, Barefoot Books, Bristol, 1999.

Ginsburg, Madeleine (ed.), *The Illustrated History of Textiles*, Studio Editions, London, 1991.

Glausiuss, Gilbert, *The Persian Carpet*, Nova Fine Art Corporation, Christchurch (New Zealand), 1981.

Harris, Jennifer (ed.), *5,000 Years of Textiles*, Harry N. Abrams, London, 1993.

Lurie, Alison, *The Language of Clothes*, Heinemann, London, 1981.

McCabe Elliot, Inger, *Batik: Fabled Cloth of Java*, Viking Penguin, London, 1984.

The Origins of String: An Interview with Elizabeth Barber (radio interview), Australian Broadcasting Corporation, 1998.

Picton, John and Mack, John, *African Textiles: Looms, Weaving and Design*, British Museum Publications, London, 1979.

Rout, Ettie A., *Maori Symbolism: Evidence of Hohepa Te Rake*, Kegan Paul, Trench, Trubner & Co, New Zealand, 1926.

Safford, Carleton L. and Bishop, Robert, *America's Quilts and Coverlets*, Studio Vista, London, 1974.

Sharaf Justin, Valerie, *Flatwoven Rugs of the World*, Van Nostrand Reinhold, New York, 1983.

Spring, Christopher, *Treasury of Decorative Art and African Textiles*, Studio, London, 1997.

Te Papa Tongarewa (the Museum of New Zealand), *Traditional Arts of Pacific Island Women* (exhibition catalog), Wellington, 1993.